the MILK FROM HOME

PARARI PUBLISHING

LCCN 2020923602

ISBN 978-1-7362462-0-7

Published by Parari Publishing
1018 Fourth Ave #206, Oakland, CA 94606
www.parari-publishing.com

the
MILK FROM HOME

Rishvika Mehta

Illustrated by Tanuja Ramani

To my parents, Uday and Smitha, who chose a harder path determined to give their daughters a life full of possibilities.

Pappa, Mummy, Rinku, and I peer at every shelf, looking for foods we used to buy back home. It's been two days since we said our sad goodbye to India. Now, we need groceries to fill the empty fridge at our new apartment.

"No garam masala!" Mummy calls out.
"Rinku, do you see any daal?" Pappa asks my sister.
She shakes her head.
I guess it's up to me to break the bad news.
"If they don't have our kind of food here, we just might have to move back," I say.
Then, I spot it.

Milk!
This is perfect. Milk and I go together like plants and water.
But wait a minute. This aisle looks like a box of crayons. Every bottle has a different cap: green, yellow, brown, and red.

When Mummy told us we were moving to America for her job, she said things wouldn't be the same here. But even the milk?
The knots in my stomach get tighter. Figuring things out in this new country is hard.

"Why do the milk bottles have different caps?" I wonder out loud.
Rinku, who's got an answer for everything, chimes in. "I bet the colors are to show that the milk is from different animals, like goats, yaks, buffaloes, and cows."
"Or maybe," I say, "the caps mean the milk is flavored, like yellow for mango."

Back home we had a mango tree as tall as a giraffe.

Mummy gathered the mangoes and sorted them into two piles: ripe and raw. She cut the ripe ones into long slices for all of us to enjoy right away. They were always sweet and juicy, leaving our hands sticky.

She chopped the raw ones into cubes and sprinkled red chilli powder all over them. This made it the tangiest, most yummiest snack.

I wish the mango tree had come with us to America.

"What do you think the colors mean?" I ask Mummy and Pappa.

They shrug.

Brrrr! I hope we figure it out soon. The cold air from the fridge is giving me goosebumps. Back home, we didn't buy milk at a store. Every night, Valli Akka, our nanny and cook, hung a basket on the front gate of our house. Then every morning, the milkman dropped two packets of cow's milk into that basket.

When she woke up, Valli Akka fetched the milk, poured it into a pot, and warmed it up before bringing Rinku and me a glass.

As we enjoyed the milk, Valli Akka sat with us and shared funny stories about the pranks she played on her two sisters.

I wish Valli Akka had come with us to America.

"There are so many to choose from. Which milk do we buy?" Rinku asks.
"Yeah," I say. "I want the milk from home."
Mummy's eyebrows dance around and finally an *ah-ha* look flashes across her face.
"Let's buy one of each," she suggests.

"One of each color?" I ask.

"Yeah, we buy them all and do a taste test to find the milk from home."

"Great idea," Pappa says.

Each of us grab a bottle with a different color cap and fill up the cart.

We race through our apartment door and settle in for the taste test.
"Hey," I say, "before we try them, let's describe the milk from home. I'll jot it down on this paper so we know what we're looking for."
"Creamy like ice cream!" Rinku says.
"Thick and heavy!" Pappa says.
"It smelled like warm butter," I add.

Just thinking about the milk from home loosens up the knots in my stomach a bit.
"Sounds like there's more to milk than just taste," Mummy says. "The texture and smell matter, too."
"Yeah!" I say, "Now that we know what we're looking for, let's start."

	TASTE	TEXTURE	SMELL
milk from home	creamy ice-cream	thick & heavy	warm butter

First up, green.
Mummy pops the bottle cap off and pours the milk into four glasses.
We each take a whiff and then a sip.
"It's got a delicate sweetish smell," Mummy says.
"It's kind of fruity," Pappa adds.

"Feels silky smooth," Rinku says, "like one of Mummy's fancy saris."
When my tongue touches the milk, it jumps back at the sugary taste.
"Ick! It's like old coconut water," I say. "Green is all wrong."

	TASTE	TEXTURE	SMELL
milk from home	creamy like ice-cream	thick & heavy	like warm butter
green	like old coconut water	silky smooth	delicate sweet fruitish

Yellow is next.
"It smells like wet mud," Rinku says.
"Oooh!" Mummy says. "It's got a nutty taste."
"Frothy," Pappa adds. "Almost like cotton candy."

The foamy milk fills my mouth with tiny bubbles. "It isn't bad," I say. "Definitely creamy, but not thick enough. Yellow isn't right either."

	TASTE	TEXTURE	SMELL
milk from home	creamy ice-cream	thick & heavy	warm butter
green	old coconut water	silky smooth	delicate sweet fruitish
yellow	nutty taste	frothy cotton candy	wet mud

Third try, brown.

The smooth, slippery milk coats my tongue with a chocolatey taste.

"I knew one of these had to be flavored!" I say. "This milk tastes like a melted chocolate bar."

Rinku smacks her lips after a sip. "And it's syrupy!"

"It smells extra chocolatey, too," Mummy adds.

"It's like a dessert," Pappa says.

"Yummy," I say, "but brown is not it."

	TASTE	TEXTURE	SMELL
milk from home	creamy ice-cream	thick & heavy	warm butter
green	old coconut water	silky smooth	delicate sweet fruitish
yellow	nutty taste	frothy cotton candy	wet mud
brown	melted chocolate	syrupy	chocolatey

There's only one more left: red.

"Cross your fingers," I say. "If this one is not like the milk from home, there's no point unpacking."

Once again, we take a whiff and then a sip.

"Oh so very creamy," Pappa says.

"It's definitely thick," Mummy adds.

"I'm getting that buttery fragrance, too," Rinku says.

I take a deep sniff before sipping the milk, and...

Gulp!

	TASTE	TEXTURE	SMELL
milk from home	creamy ice-cream	thick & heavy	warm butter
green	old coconut water	silky smooth	delicate sweet fruitish
yellow	nutty taste	frothy cotton candy	wet mud
brown	melted chocolate	syrupy	chocolatey
red	creamy	thick	buttery fragrance

Buttery smell, check!
Creamy, check!
Thick, check!
"Red should be the one," I say. "But something is missing. What is it?"

I close my eyes and think about drinking milk in India.

Valli Akka woke up.
She fetched the milk from the basket.
Then she poured it into a pot...
"This milk is cold!" I shout.
"Huh?" Pappa says.
"We need to warm up the milk like Vallii Akka did!"

We rush to the microwave.
"How much time should I set it for?" I ask.
"3 minutes?" Pappa guesses.
"That might be too long," Mummy says.
"1 minute," Rinku says.
I press 1, 0, 0, and Start.
BEEP. BEEP. BEEP. It's ready!

We reach into the microwave and grab our glasses. Pappa, Mummy, and Rinku take a sip. Right away, their faces light up.

I hold the glass in my hands, breathing in the buttery scent that comes from the steam. Then I take a big sip.

As the warm milk washes down my throat, the knots in my stomach finally untangle. This milk smells, feels, and tastes just right.

"What do you think?" Mummy asks.

"Don't make us wait all day," Rinku says.

Pappa plays a drum roll with his fingers on the counter.

"I guess we can unpack after all," I say. "We found the milk from home!"

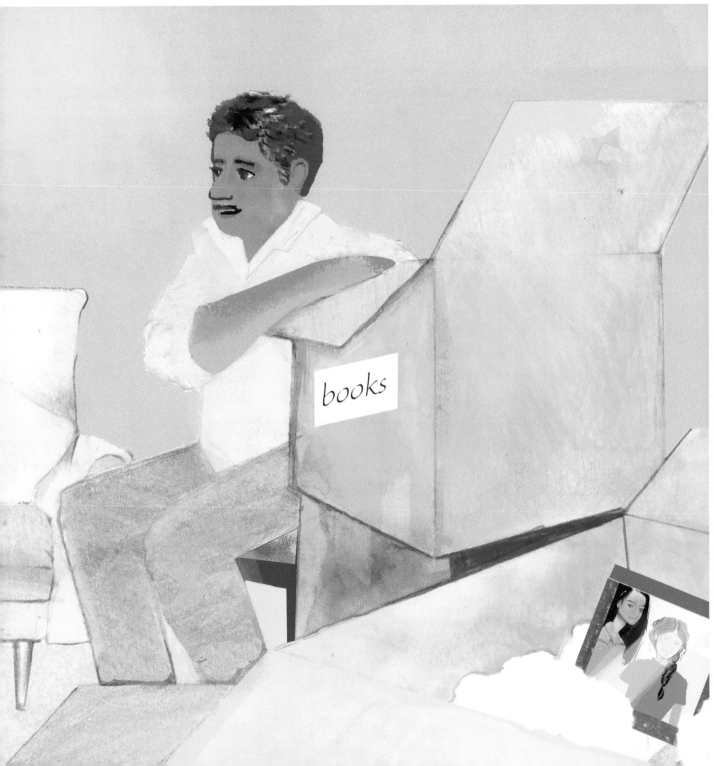

ABOUT THE AUTHOR

Rishvika Kumar Mehta immigrated to California in 1997 as a curious, quick-witted, and straight-talking nine year old. She's always been drawn to the craft of storytelling, and was inspired to become an author when she learned about the lack of diversity in children's books. Rishvika is happiest when she's curled up on the couch with her husband, Jatin, and dog, Henri.

ABOUT THE ILLUSTRATOR

Tanuja Ramani spent hours on end escaping into picture books as a child, many of them have had a great and lasting impact on her creativity. When working on her art, Tanuja draws inspiration from people, places, and the natural world. You'll find Tanuja hanging out in Chennai, India with her husband, Siddharth, and cats.

CPSIA information can be obtained
at www.ICGtesting.com
Printed in the USA
BVHW021426310821
615283BV00003B/5